The Gift of Mittens

By

Kimberly Manganelli

Illustrated By

Debra Tielman

Ordering Information:

For details, contact Kim@kimberlymanganelli.com

www.kimberlymanganelli.com

Edited by Lauren Lohman; illustrated by Debra Tielman

Print ISBN: 978-1-66780-783-6

Printed in the United States of America

First Edition

In memory of my grandmother, who inspired this story. She always helped all of God's creatures. One day she found an abused cat at her doorstep. She nursed him back to health and gave him a safe home and all the love in her heart.

I love you Gram.
Kim

"Whoosh, whoosh," whispered the grass in the vast fields all around.
"Thump, thump. Thump, thump," went Mittens' heart, in a loud sound.

The sunlight cascaded like water from a spout
and magically erased any sign of his doubt.
He swallowed the lump in the back of his dry throat,
then took off like the wind behind the sail of a boat.

The black on his front paws was as dark as the night.
The white on his legs and body was bright like a light.
Mittens traveled the streets with true aspiration,
his four little paws his source of transportation.

With footsteps of purpose and his heart as a guide,
there was no doubt, good luck was on Mittens' side.
He imagined a much better place to be.
He had left his cruel owners and decided to flee.

One day on his journey, he met a snowball of white.
The fluffy, furry dog greeted the cat with delight.
"My name is Buster. Hello there, my fine friend indeed!
How can I help you? What is it that you need?"

"Pleased to meet you. My name is Mittens. How do you do?"
Buster answered, "Nice to meet you.
The pleasure is mine.
Now what is it, Mittens, that I can help you find?"

Mittens uttered, "I've been searching for a home that feels *purrfectly* right.
A loving home that is safe all day and all night."
Buster replied, "Okay. I have a solution.
I have something to add to make a great contribution."

"Go past the peaceful village and there on the right,
is a little red house lit up with a light.
In it lives a lady who is as kind as can be.
She is sweet as sugar, all would agree."
Mittens nodded, thanked him, and headed on his way.
Buster cheered, "Goodbye, ciao, arrivederci, good day!"

Mittens headed along trusting faith as his sight.
The stars in the sky revealed the magic of twilight.
With music in his heart and desire in his soul,
his every step was automatic, as if on cruise control.

He strolled around a slight bend when something stopped him again.
It was the cruel, awful dog, Meanie Max.
Here was another adventure, just as he was beginning to relax.
Mittens peered over and noticed a kitten shaking with fright.

He knew, at that moment, something was not right.
"Give me all of your milk!" Meanie Max demanded.
The kitty whined, "I'm thirsty. Please, I need to have some."
"No! You will certainly not," barked Max. "You are done!"

Mittens thought for a moment, then knew what to do.
Standing up to bullies was something he knew.
Mittens growled, howled, and meowed with all his migh
Within minutes, Buster and his friends were in sight.

Frankie, the fox, sprinted all the way from the railroad tracks.
Then, he stared long and hard at the bully, Meanie Max.
Like a flash, in swooped Carina, the cawing crow.
From a branch, "Caw, caw, caw," radiated below.

Next, in crept Mary Jo, the bold calico
Her giant green eyes expressed her wo
Out bolted Buster, the spunky bichor
as fast as a mischievous leprechaun.

Every animal came out with Mittens' loud cry—
even Salvador, the bulldog, in his new bow tie.
Bella, the collie, bustled on to the scene.
United together, their presence taught Max to stop being mean.

With a pack of animals on Mittens' side,
Suddenly, Meanie Max became almost clear-eyed.
He took a step back and hung his head low.
Then, after a while, he turned around real slow.

He looked up as one single tear dropped from his eye.
He turned back around and mumbled, "Sorry. Goodbye."

Mittens thanked his fine friends who came to his call.
He knew there was a way to help, even if he too was small.
Mittens remembered a message he had learned when he was young,
a lesson he learned when his life had just begun.

His mama had taught him to assist others in their time of need.
However, she had explained, it may take a few friends to succeed.
Her words of insightful wisdom sure helped this day.
It sure helped them make Meanie Max go away.

Mittens scurried off to continue his crusade.
Hours had passed. He paused and glanced up at the trees as they swayed.
They whispered a message, "Keep going, always persevere.
You'll be there before long. You are so very near."

Shortly after, he passed the village, and there on the right
was the magical house lit up by a light.
At last, he found it—it just had to be.
Right in front of his eyes, it was a sight to see.

From a distance, he saw a lady rocking in a chair.
He had an instant feeling they'd make a great pair.
Her long blond hair was wrapped up in a bun,
in a perfect circle with golden streaks like the sun.

Mittens graciously walked right up to the door
He meowed and meowed, then meowed some mo
The little old lady looked up from her book,
then peered out the window to take a quick loo

Next, she walked slowly and creaked open the door.
She looked down to see precious Mittens on the floor.
Her adoring heart filled with happiness and delight.
They both were very joyous that marvelous night.

She picked up Mittens and gave him a gentle squeeze,
Then stated, "I'll take care of you. My name is Berniece.
I will always love you with all of my heart."
Mittens knew from that moment they were off to a great star

Berniece sat down, then rocked back and forth in her chair.
Then, she looked up, clasped her hands together, and exclaimed,
"Thank you, thank you, thank you for answering my prayer!"

Mittens curled up in her lap. Finally, he could rest.
They both felt extremely fortunate and so very blessed.
A sweeping smile came across the dear face of Berniece.
They both were fast asleep and got plenty of zzzzz.